For Emily Elizabeth, my littlest granddaughter

Copyright © 1995 by John Schoenherr. All rights reserved. This book, or parts thereof, may not be reproduced in any form without permission in writing from the publisher. Philomel Books, a division of The Putnam & Grosset Group, 200 Madison Avenue, New York, NY 10016. Philomel Books, Reg. U.S. Pat. & Tm. Off. Published simultaneously in Canada. Printed in Hong Kong by South China Printing Co. (1988) Ltd. Book design by Donna Mark. The text is set in Horley Old Style. Library of Congress Cataloging-in-Publication Data. Schoenherr, John. Rebel / by John Schoenherr.   p.   cm. Summary: A pair of geese build a nest and raise their goslings until they all fly south together. 1. Geese—Juvenile fiction.   [1. Geese—Fiction.] I. Title. PZ10.3.S29894Re 1995 [E]—dc20 94-15568 CIP AC ISBN 0-399-22727-X 10 9 8 7 6 5 4 3 2 1   First Impression

John Schoenherr

REBEL

Philomel Books   New York

The wild geese come when the ice starts
to melt, and fly to their very own pond.

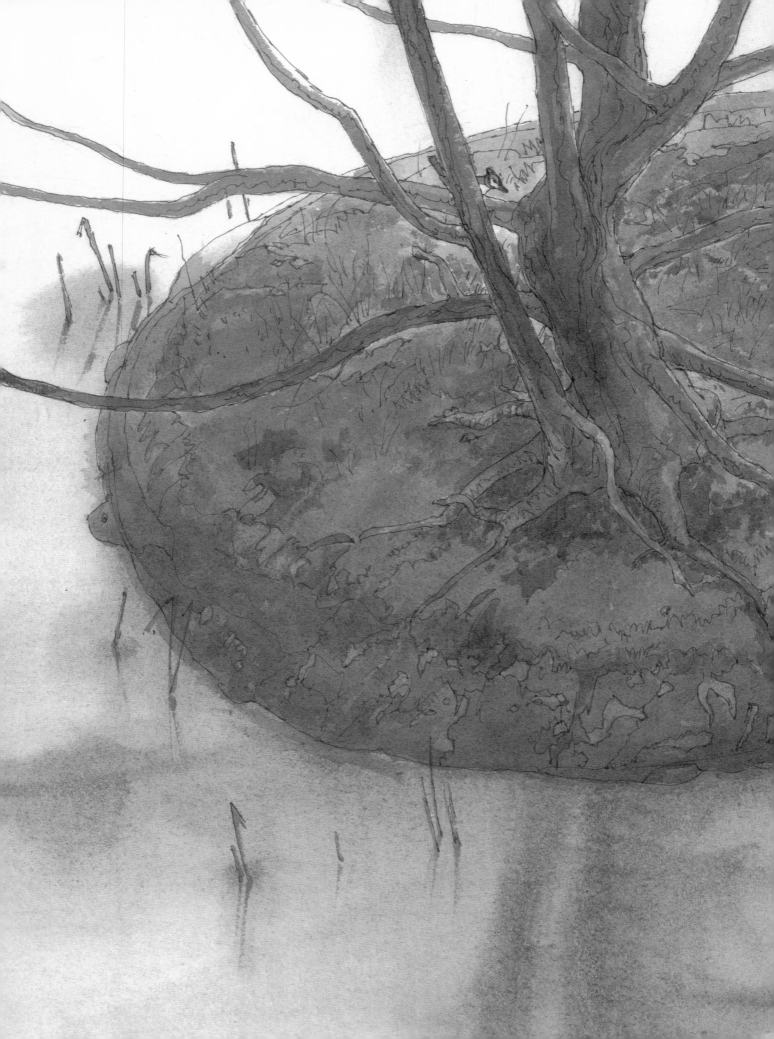

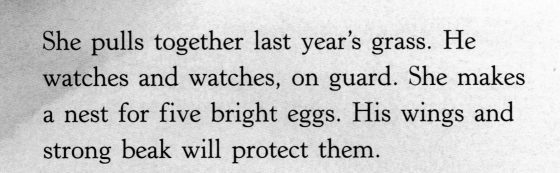

She pulls together last year's grass. He
watches and watches, on guard. She makes
a nest for five bright eggs. His wings and
strong beak will protect them.

She covers the eggs with down from her breast and settles gently on top. He watches and guards through the days and the nights, never going far.

Through chilling rain and blowing wind
she sits and sits and sits.

She leaves to eat, but comes right back.
And sits and sits and sits.

Then the eggs start to peep and the shells
start to crack. New goslings break into the
world.

The world is cold, but the nest is warm.
They huddle close under their mother.

They nibble tender blades of grass and
juicy shoots of weeds. As close as peas they
stay together, never going far.

Like one bird they swim together, eating
all they can.

They're warm and fed and safe all day.
Dark night is time to sleep.

Parents guard them through the night.

They keep them safe and close.

When morning comes, they'll leave the pond and won't come back this year.

They'll go together to a brooding ground,
where all the families gather.

There they'll stay till all can fly.
And all fly south together.